Bravo Phonics

Cecilia Chan

Level 3

The Commercial Press

Edited by: Betty Wong

Cover designed by: Cathy Chiu

Typeset by: Rong Zhou

Printing arranged by: Kenneth Lung

Bravo Phonics (Level 3)

Author: Cecilia Chan

Publisher: The Commercial Press (H.K.) Ltd.

8/F, Eastern Central Plaza, 3 Yiu Hing Road, Shau Kei Wan, H.K.

http://www.commercialpress.com.hk

Distributor: THE SUP Publishing Logistics (H.K.) Ltd.

16/F, Tsuen Wan Industrial Building, 220-248 Texaco Road,

Tsuen Wan, NT, Hong Kong

Printer: Elegance Printing and Book Binding Co., Ltd.

Block A, 4/F, Hoi Bun Industrial Building 6 Wing Yip Street,

Kwun Tung Kowloon, Hong Kong

© 2023 The Commercial Press (H.K.) Ltd.

First edition, First printing, July 2023

ISBN 978 962 07 0622 6

Printed in Hong Kong

Bravo Phonics Series is a special gift to all children - the ability to READ ENGLISH accurately and fluently! ENJOY!

About the Author

The author, Ms Cecilia Chan, is a well-known English educator with many years of teaching experience. Passionate and experienced in teaching English, Ms Chan has taught students from over 30 schools in Hong Kong, including Marymount Primary School, Marymount Secondary School, Diocesan Boys' School, Diocesan Girls' School, St. Paul's Co-educational College, St. Paul's Co-educational College Primary School, St. Paul's College, St. Paul's Convent School (Primary and Secondary Sections), Belilios Public School, Raimondi College Primary Section, St. Clare's Primary School, St. Joseph's Primary School, St. Joseph's College, Pun U Association Wah Yan Primary School and other international schools. Many of Ms Chan's students have won prizes in Solo Verse Speaking, Prose Reading and Public Speaking at the Hong Kong Schools Speech Festival and

other interschool open speech contests. Driven by her passion in promoting English learning, Ms Chan has launched the Bravo Phonics Series (Levels I-5) as an effective tool to foster a love of English reading and learning in children.

To all my Beloved Students

Acknowledgement

Many thanks to the Editor, JY Ho, for her effort and contribution to the editing of the Bravo Phonics Series and her assistance all along.

Author's Words

The fundamental objective of phonics teaching is to develop step-by-step a child's ability to pronounce and recognize the words in the English language. Each phonic activity is a means to build up the child's power of word recognition until such power has been thoroughly exercised that word recognition becomes practically automatic.

Proper phonic training is highly important to young children especially those with English as a second language. It enables a child to acquire a large reading vocabulary in a comparatively short time and hence can happily enjoy fluent story reading. By giving phonics a place in the daily allotment of children's activities, they can be brought to a state of reading proficiency at an early age. Be patient, allow ample time for children to enjoy each and every phonic activity; if it is well and truly done, further steps will be taken easily and much more quickly.

Bravo Phonics Series has proven to be of value in helping young children reach the above objective and embark joyfully on the voyage of learning to read. It consists of five books of five levels, covering all the letter sounds of the consonants,

short and long vowels, diphthongs and blends in the English language. Bravo Phonics Series employs a step-by-step approach, integrating different learning skills through a variety of fun reading, writing, drawing, spelling and story-telling activities. There are quizzes, drills, tongue twisters, riddles and comprehension exercises to help consolidate all the letter sounds learnt. The QR code on each page enables a child to self-learn at home by following the instructions of Ms Chan while simultaneously practising the letter sounds through the example given.

The reward to teachers and parents will be a thousandfold when children gain self-confidence and begin to apply their phonic experiences to happy story reading.

Contents

Quick Guide

Read

Write

Scan

Colour

Circle

Draw

 Say

ABC Spell

Check

Cross Out

Join

Hello, this is Ms Chan. How are you?
Are you ready to learn Bravo Phonics?
Let's learn about Consonant Sounds!

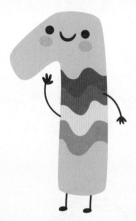

Initial Consonant Sounds

g

w

k

j

Initial Consonant Sounds

 Say the names of the pictures.

 Circle the correct sound with which each picture begins.

g j k w   **w j k g**   **j k g w**

g k w j   **k g w j**

 Say the names of the pictures after me.

 Now colour the pictures.

2

Say the names of the pictures.

 Write the sound with which each picture begins on the line.

_____ _____ _____

_____ _____

 Say the names of the pictures after me.

 Now colour the pictures.

3

Initial Consonant Sounds

 Say the names of the pictures.

 Circle the word that matches each picture.

king	grass	witch
kite	grapes	wing
kid	green	wish

kettle	jaw
kitten	jelly
key	jug

 Say the names of the pictures after me.

 Now colour the pictures.

4

Say the names of the pictures.

 Spell the name of each picture by writing the sound with which the picture begins.

_____oose   _____ump   _____ick

_____oldfish   _____atch

 Spell and say the names of the pictures after me.

 Now colour the pictures.

5

Let's learn about Vowel Sounds!

Vowel Sounds

a e i o u

Vowel Sounds

 Say the names of the pictures.

 Circle the correct sound with which each picture begins.

 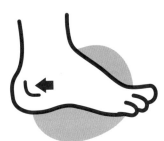 

aeiou **eioua** **ouiea**

eaiou **uiaoe**

 Say the names of the pictures after me.

  Now colour the pictures.

8

Say the names of the pictures.

 Circle the correct sound with which each picture begins.

aeiou   **eioua**   **ouiea**

eaiou   **uiaoe**

 Say the names of the pictures after me.

 Now colour the pictures.

q

Vowel Sounds

 Say the words in each box after me.

 Write on the line the word that tells about each picture.

man hen pig fox rug	

mug wig cop rat ten	

dog mat fit tub web	

den bib hat jug pot	

 Say the correct words after me.

  Now colour the pictures.

10

Say the words in each box after me.

 Write on the line the word that tells about each picture.

| bat |
| cub |
| log |
| kid |
| bed |

_____

| peg |
| sun |
| lid |
| fan |
| dot |

_____

| pen |
| tip |
| cup |
| cot |
| map |

_____

| box |
| cut |
| pet |
| tap |
| six |

_____

 Say the correct words after me.

 Now colour the pictures.

11

Let's learn more Consonant Sounds!

Final Consonant Sounds

b   l

d   ss

g   ll

k   ff

Final Consonant Sounds

 Say the first sound.

 Circle one of the other sounds to build the word that matches the picture.

 Write the word on the line.

bi(g k b)   be(l d b)

_____   _____

hu(k g l)   des(l d k)

_____   _____

 Say the names of the pictures after me.

 Now colour the pictures.

14

Say the first sound.

 Circle one of the other sounds to build the word that matches the picture.

 Write the word on the line.

bi(ss ll ff)

_____

ki(ff ll ss)

_____

we(ll ss ff)

_____

pu(ss ff ll)

_____

 Say the names of the pictures after me.

 Now colour the pictures.

15

Rhyming Words are fun!
Are you ready for the challenge?
Let's begin!

Rhyming Words

Rhyming Words

 Say the words in each box.

 Circle those words that rhyme with the first one.

kill   gill   tell

will   ball

tuff   moss   muff

ruff   puff

18

loss bell boss wall toss

hall tall fall muff call

tell fell bell well ball

 Now say the words that rhyme after me.

Rhyming Words

 Say the words in each box.

 Circle those words that rhyme with the first one.

man   pan   men   fan   bad

nod   fat   rod   cod   pod

20

bib nib rib
dim bet

nail sail fail
lap tail

beg rag peg
leg gut

 Now say the words that rhyme after me.

Rhyming Words

 Say the words in each box after me.

 Cross out the words that do not tell about each picture.

sand
land
hand

rent
lent
tent

fist
list
mist

lift
sift
gift

 Say the names of the pictures after me.

 Now colour the pictures.

22

Say the words in each box after me.

 Cross out the words that do not tell about the picture.

felt
melt
belt

band
sand
hand

silk
bilk
milk

camp
lamp
damp

 Say the names of the pictures after me.

 Now colour the pictures.

23

Rhyming Words

 Say the words in each box.

 Circle those words that rhyme with the first one.

bend mend send sent lend

test rest desk best nest

mint tent tint hint milk

rift sift rest gift lift

felt tent melt belt send

 Now say the words that rhyme after me.

Rhyming Words

 Say the words in each box.

 Circle those words that rhyme with the first one.

talk walk chalk
lock silk

camp lamp lamb
damp ramp

26

pond send bond
fond land

dust must mist
gust rust

rent sent bent
tend tent

 Now say the words that rhyme after me.

Rhyming Words

 Say the words in each box after me.

 Cross out the words that do not tell about each picture.

task

cask

mask

buck

duck

suck

king

sing

ring

tank

sank

bank

 Say the names of the pictures after me.

 Now colour the pictures.

28

Say the words in each box after me.

 Cross out the words that do not tell about each picture.

night
right
might

dish
fish
wish

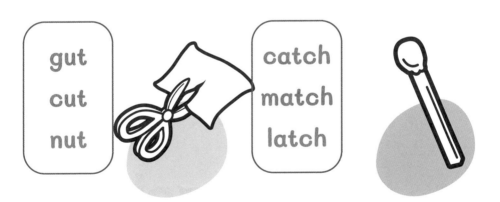

gut
cut
nut

catch
match
latch

 Say the names of the pictures after me.

 Now colour the pictures.

29

Rhyming Words

 Say the words in each box.

 Circle those words that rhyme with the first one.

ask mask disk
task cask

sack peck rack
tack pack

bang ring rang
sang back

rink sink sank
link ling

tight sigh light
sight tint

Now say the words that rhyme after me.

31

Rhyming Words

 Say the words in each box.

 Circle those words that rhyme with the first one.

dash mash cash
rash task

fits sits dots
bits hits

ditch fetch hitch hatch fitch

light fight right limp might

sock lock lack mock rock

 Now say the words that rhyme after me.

Are you ready for the Quizzes?
Let's start!

Quizzes

Join each picture with the word that tells about it.

• nest

• lift

• band

• bent

 •

• jump

 •

• suck

 •

• melt

 •

• desk

 Now say the names of the pictures after me.

 Score /8

37

Join each picture with the word that tells about it.

 •

• **tank**

 •

• **touch**

 •

• **ring**

 •

• **wash**

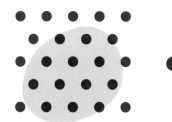 • • camp

 • • catch

 • • dots

 • • fight

 Now say the names of the pictures after me.

 Score /8

39

Choose a word from the list that rhymes with the words in each row.

 Write the word on the line.

| last | mend | lift | punt |

send   bend   _____

hunt   runt   _____

fast   cast   _____

sift   gift   _____

40

 Now say the words that rhyme after me.

Score

/4

Choose a word from the list that rhymes with the words in each row.

 Write the word on the line.

| touch | sink | bang | mask |

task   bask   _____

gang   hang   _____

link   rink   _____

such   much   _____

 Now say the words that rhyme after me.

Score

/4

41

Choose a word from the list that rhymes with the words in each row.

 Write the word on the line.

talk	king	sock	camp

sing   ring   _____

walk   chalk   _____

damp   tramp   _____

mock   clock   _____

 Now say the words that rhyme after me.

Score

/4

Choose a word from the list that rhymes with the words in each row.

 Write the word on the line.

| tents | match | cash | night |

lash   trash   _____

rents   cents   _____

catch   latch   _____

might   fight   _____

 Now say the words that rhyme after me.

Score

/4

43

Are you ready for the challenge?
Let's begin!

Say and Draw

Say and Draw

 Say the words in each box after me.

 Draw a picture of what you read in each box.

 Colour your pictures.

A handbag

46

A playground

A dustbin

Say and Draw

 Say the words in each box after me.

 Draw a picture of what you read in each box.

 Colour your pictures.

A big doll

A fat pig

A long belt

Say and Draw

 Say the words in each box after me.

 Draw a picture of what you read in each box.

 Colour your pictures.

A fish on a dish

50

A pen on a desk

A finger with a ring

Say and Draw

 Say the words in each box after me.

 Draw a picture of what you read in each box.

 Colour your pictures.

A drum and two drum sticks

A trap to catch a rat

A big clock on a rock

Say and Draw

 Say the words in each box after me.

 Draw a picture of what you read in each box.

 Colour your pictures.

Two ducks on a pond

54

Three tents in a camp

Four eggs in a nest

Riddles are fun! Are you ready
for the challenge? Let's begin!

Riddles

Riddles

 Read the sentence in each box after me.

 Guess what it is in each box and draw it.

 Colour your pictures.

It tells the time.

58

We sleep on it.

We swim in it.

Riddles

 Read the sentence in each box after me.

 Guess what it is in each box and draw it.

 Colour your pictures.

We need it when it rains.

We use it to catch fish.

We get it from the bank.

Riddles

 Read the sentence in each box after me.

 Guess what it is in each box and draw it.

 Colour your pictures.

He wears a crown.

It lives in the sea.

We beat it to make sounds.

Let's learn more Consonant Sounds!

Initial Consonants Sounds

y

v

z

qu

y

 Say the names of the pictures.

 Write the sound with which each picture begins on the line.

 Say the names of the pictures after me.

y
_____   _____

_____   _____

 Write the sound 'y'.

 Say it aloud as you write it.

Y y Y y Y y

 Now colour the pictures.

67

Say the names of the pictures.

Circle those pictures which begin with the sound 'y'.

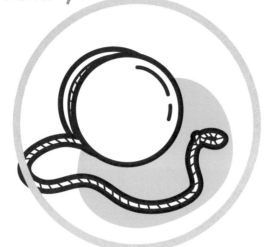

y

68

y

 Say the names of the pictures which begin with the sound 'y' after me.

 Now colour the pictures which begin with the sound 'y'.

V

Say the names of the pictures.

Write the sound with which each picture begins on the line.

Say the names of the pictures after me.

V

_____   _____

_____   _____

 Write the sound 'v'.

 Say it aloud as you write it.

V v V v V v

 Now colour the pictures.

71

V

Say the names of the pictures.

Circle those pictures which begin with the sound 'v'.

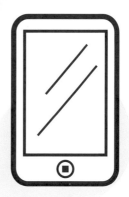

 Say the names of the pictures which begin with the sound 'v' after me.

 Now colour the pictures which begin with the sound 'v'.

73

Z

Say the names of the pictures.

Write the sound with which each picture begins on the line.

Say the names of the pictures after me.

2-2 =

z

_____   _____

_____   _____

 Write the sound 'z'.

 Say it aloud as you write it.

Z z   Z z   Z z

Now colour the pictures.

Z

Say the names of the pictures.

Circle those pictures which begin with the sound 'z'.

2-2 =

Z

z

 Say the names of the pictures which begin with the sound 'z' after me.

 Now colour the pictures which begin with the sound 'z'.

77

qu

 Say the names of the pictures.

 Write the sound with which each picture begins on the line.

 Say the names of the pictures after me.

qu _____ _____

_____ _____

Write the sound 'qu'.

 Say it aloud as you write it.

Qu qu Qu qu

 Now colour the pictures.

79

qu

Say the names of the pictures.

Circle those pictures which begin with the sound 'qu'.

qu

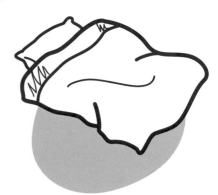

qu

 Say the names of the pictures which begin with the sound 'qu' after me.

 Now colour the pictures which begin with the sound 'qu'.

Let's learn more Consonant Sounds!

Final Consonants Sounds

x

Say the names of the pictures.

Write the sound with which each picture ends on the line.

Say the names of the pictures after me.

X

_____

_____

84

_____

_____

Write the sound 'x'.

 Say it aloud as you write it.

 X x X x X x

 Now colour the pictures.

Say the names of the pictures.

Circle those pictures which end with the sound 'x'.

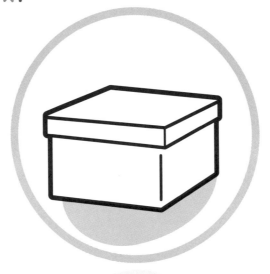

 Say the names of the pictures which end with the sound 'x' after me.

 Now colour the pictures which end with the sound 'x'.

87

Are you ready for more Quizzes?
Let's begin!

Quizzes

SCAN ME

 Say the names of the pictures.

 Circle the correct sound with which each picture begins.

y v z qu   v qu y z   z qu v y

v z qu y   y v z qu   qu y z v

90

 Now say the names of the pictures after me.

Score

/6

Say the names of the pictures.

 Write the sound with which each picture begins on the line.

_____   _____   _____

_____   _____   _____

 Now say the names of the pictures after me.

 Score /6

Quiz 10.3

 Say the names of the pictures.

 Write the sound with which each picture begins on the line.

qu
_____   _____   _____

_____   _____   _____

 Now say the names of the pictures after me.

92

Score
/6

Quiz 10.4

 Say the names of the pictures.

 Circle the word that matches each picture.

fan   lawn   get

(van)   yawn   vet

ran   prawn   wet

 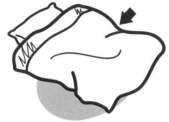 

yellow   quilt   tip

fellow   kilt   lip

mellow   tilt   zip

 Now say the names of the pictures after me.

Score /6

93

Quiz 10.5

Say the names of the pictures.

Circle the word that matches each picture.

ox
box
fox

fix
six
mix

folk
talk
yolk

seen
keen
queen

rack
quack
sack

zoo
boo
poo

Now say the names of the pictures after me.

94

Score

/6

Say the names of the pictures.

 Spell the name of each picture by filling in the missing sound.

_____an _____ipper _____olk

_____ox _____ox

 Spell and say the names of the pictures after me.

Score

/5

95

Say the names of the pictures.

 Spell the name of each picture by filling in the missing sound.

_____iolin _____o-yo ____ ____een

_____x _____et

 Spell and say the names of the pictures after me.

96

Score

/5

Say the names of the pictures.

 Spell the name of each picture by filling in the missing sound.

2-2 =

_____awn   _____ero   _____ase

_____ _____ack   _____oo

 Spell and say the names of the pictures after me.

Score

/5

97

Say the names of the pictures.

 Spell the name of each picture by filling in the missing sound.

_____ebra   _____ell   _____ _____ilt

_____-ray   _____oghurt

 Spell and say the names of the pictures after me.

Score

/5

Are you ready for more practice?
Let's begin!

Read and Match

Read and Match

Read the words on the right.

Join each picture with the words that tell about it.

a zebra running

a man yawning

a boy playing the violin

 •

•  **a vet and a dog**

 •

• **a queen with a mask**

 •

• **six socks in a box**

 Say the words after me.

 Now colour the pictures.

Read and Match

Read the words on the right.

Join each picture with the words that tell about it.

nine
• question marks

two boys
• playing yo-yos

five egg-
• yolks on a plate

a woman cooking vegetables

three lions in a zoo

four vases on a table

 Say the words after me.

 Now colour the pictures.

Are you ready for more challenges?
Let's start!

Read and Draw

Read and Draw

 Read the words in each box after me.

 Draw as you are told to do.

 Colour your pictures.

This is a cave.
Draw a fox in it.

108

There is a match in the box.
Draw three more matches in it.

Read and Draw

 Read the words in each box after me.

 Draw as you are told to do.

 Colour your pictures.

It is raining.
Draw an umbrella for the man.

It is sunny.
Draw two birds flying in the sky.

Read and Draw

 Read the words in each box after me.

 Draw as you are told to do.

 Colour your pictures.

Ann is very hungry.
Draw a hotdog on her plate.

Mother gives a bike to Tom.
Draw Tom riding on it.

Read and Draw

 Read the words in each box after me.

 Draw as you are told to do.

 Colour your pictures.

This is a doll.
Colour her dress orange
and her hair yellow.

This is a clown.
Colour his nose red
and his hair green.

Riddles are fun! Are you ready for the challenge? Let's begin!

Riddles

Riddles

 Read the sentences in each box after me.

 Guess the animal riddle and draw the answer in the box.

 Spell the name of the animal and write it on the lines.

 Colour your pictures.

a _____ _____ _____

It has big eyes and a long tail.
It says, "Meow, meow!"

118

a _____ _____ _____ _____
It swims on a pond.
It says, "Quack, quack!"

Riddles

 Read the sentences in each box after me.

 Guess the animal riddle and draw the answer in the box.

 Spell the name of the animal and write it on the lines.

 Colour your pictures.

SCAN ME

a ____ ____ ____

It loves honey.
It says, "Buzz, buzz!"

a _____ _____ _____

It lays eggs.

It sits on her eggs in a nest.

Riddles

 Read the sentences in each box after me.

 Guess the animal riddle and draw the answer in the box.

 Spell the name of the animal and write it on the lines.

 Colour your pictures.

a ____ ____ ____ ____ ____

It has four legs.
It is strong and fast. We
can ride on it.

a _____ _____ _____ _____
It has a green skin.
It can jump and swim in the
pond.

Are you ready for more challenges?
Let's start!

Let's think

Let's think

Read each question after me and circle the correct answer.

Can a bee buzz?	**Yes**	**No**
Can a pig fly?	**Yes**	**No**
Does a hen lay eggs?	**Yes**	**No**
Does a fox say "Quack, quack"?	**Yes**	**No**
Can we smell a rose?	**Yes**	**No**
Can we cut with silk?	**Yes**	**No**
Do we sleep on the wall?	**Yes**	**No**
Does the queen wear a crown?	**Yes**	**No**

Now let's check the answers.

126

Read each question after me and

 circle the correct answer.

Can we cook in a vase?   **Yes**   **No**

Can we see tents in a camp?   **Yes**   **No**

Do we play music in a band?   **Yes**   **No**

Do we keep fish in a bank?   **Yes**   **No**

Is a lion bigger than a horse?   **Yes**   **No**

Are there elephants in a zoo?   **Yes**   **No**

Will ice melt in the sun?   **Yes**   **No**

Will plants grow without water?   **Yes**   **No**

Now let's check the answers.

Well done, students! You can check your answers with the Answer Key.

Answer Key

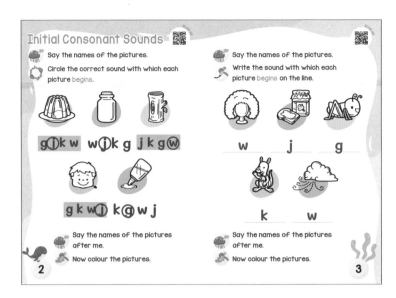

Initial Consonant Sounds

Say the names of the pictures.

Circle the correct sound with which each picture begins.

g **j** k w   w **j** k g **w**

g k w **j**   k **g** w j

Say the names of the pictures after me.

Now colour the pictures.

2

Say the names of the pictures.

Write the sound with which each picture begins on the line.

w   j   g

k   w

Say the names of the pictures after me.

Now colour the pictures.

3

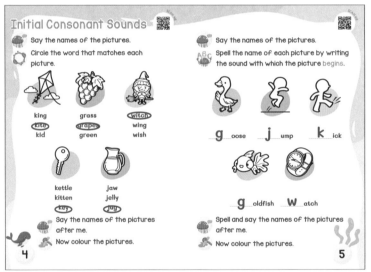

Initial Consonant Sounds

Say the names of the pictures.

Circle the word that matches each picture.

king   grass   witch
kite   **grapes**   wing
kid   green   wish

kettle   jaw
kitten   jelly
key   **jug**

Say the names of the pictures after me.

Now colour the pictures.

4

Say the names of the pictures.

Spell the name of each picture by writing the sound with which the picture begins.

g oose   **j** ump   **k** ick

g oldfish   **w** atch

Spell and say the names of the pictures after me.

Now colour the pictures.

5

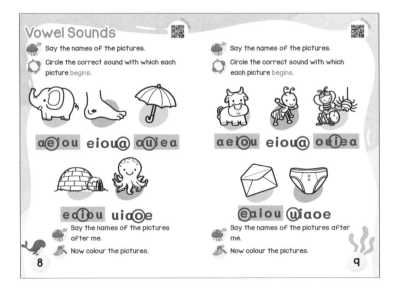

Vowel Sounds

Say the names of the pictures.

Circle the correct sound with which each picture begins.

a **e** i o u   e i o u **a**   o **u** i e a

e **a** i o u   u i a **o** e

Say the names of the pictures after me.

Now colour the pictures.

8

Say the names of the pictures.

Circle the correct sound with which each picture begins.

a e i **o** u   e i o u **a**   o **u** i e a

e a i o u   **u** i a o e

Say the names of the pictures after me.

Now colour the pictures.

q

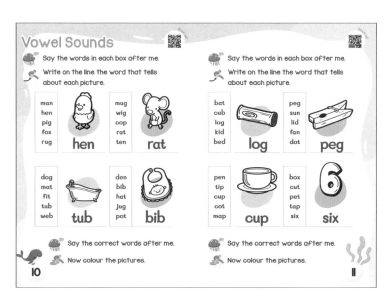

Vowel Sounds

Say the words in each box after me.

Write on the line the word that tells about each picture.

man hen pig fox rug	**hen**	mug wig cop rat ten	**rat**
dog mat fit tub web	**tub**	den bib hat jug pot	**bib**

Say the correct words after me.

Now colour the pictures.

10

Say the words in each box after me.

Write on the line the word that tells about each picture.

bat cub log kid bed	**log**	peg sun lid fan dot	**peg**
pen tip cup cot map	**cup**	box cut pet tap six	**six**

Say the correct words after me.

Now colour the pictures.

11

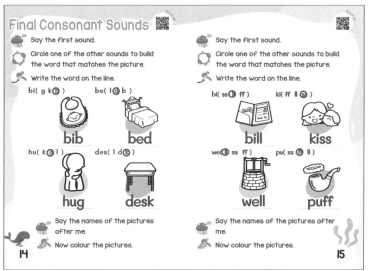

Final Consonant Sounds

Say the first sound.

Circle one of the other sounds to build the word that matches the picture.

Write the word on the line.

bi(g k (t)) be(l (d) b)

bib **bed**

hu(k (g) l) des(l d (k))

hug **desk**

Say the names of the pictures after me.

Now colour the pictures.

14

Say the first sound.

Circle one of the other sounds to build the word that matches the picture.

Write the word on the line.

bi(ss (l) ff) ki(ff ll (ss))

bill **kiss**

we((ll) ss ff) pu(ss (ff) ll)

well **puff**

Say the names of the pictures after me.

Now colour the pictures.

15

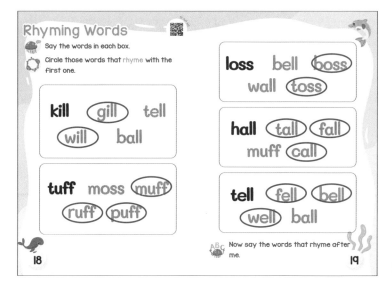

Rhyming Words

Say the words in each box.

Circle those words that rhyme with the first one.

kill (gill) tell (will) ball

tuff moss (muff) (ruff) (puff)

loss bell (boss) wall (toss)

hall (tall) (fall) muff (call)

tell (fell) (bell) (well) ball

Now say the words that rhyme after me.

18   19

131

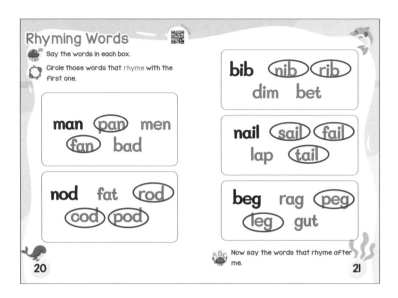

Rhyming Words

🪼 Say the words in each box.

⭕ Circle those words that rhyme with the first one.

man (pan) men (fan) bad

nod fat (rod) (cod) (pod)

bib (nib) (rib) dim bet

nail (sail) (fail) lap (tail)

beg rag (peg) (leg) gut

Now say the words that rhyme after me.

20   21

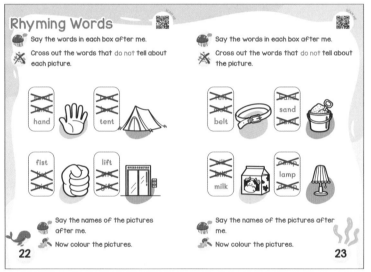

Rhyming Words

🪼 Say the words in each box after me.

✖ Cross out the words that do not tell about each picture.

hand   tent
fist   lift

Say the names of the pictures after me.

Now colour the pictures.

🪼 Say the words in each box after me.

✖ Cross out the words that do not tell about the picture.

belt   sand
milk   lamp

Say the names of the pictures after me.

Now colour the pictures.

22   23

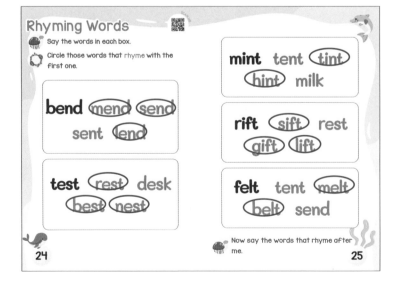

Rhyming Words

🪼 Say the words in each box.

⭕ Circle those words that rhyme with the first one.

bend (mend) (send) sent (lend)

test (rest) desk (best) (nest)

mint tent (tint) (hint) milk

rift (sift) rest (gift) (lift)

felt tent (melt) (belt) send

Now say the words that rhyme after me.

24   25

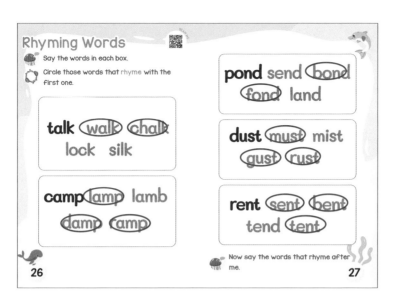

Rhyming Words

Say the words in each box.

Circle those words that rhyme with the first one.

talk (walk) (chalk) lock silk

camp (lamp) lamb (damp) (camp)

pond send (bond) (fond) land

dust (must) mist (gust) (rust)

rent (sent) (bent) tend (tent)

Now say the words that rhyme after me.

26

27

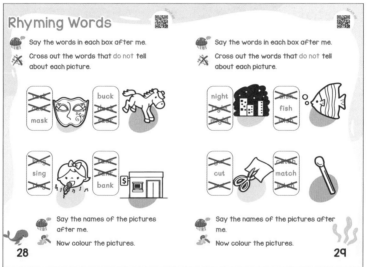

Rhyming Words

Say the words in each box after me.

Cross out the words that do not tell about each picture.

mask ~~buck~~

~~sing~~ bank

night ~~fish~~

~~cut~~ ~~match~~

Say the names of the pictures after me.

Now colour the pictures.

Say the names of the pictures after me.

Now colour the pictures.

28

29

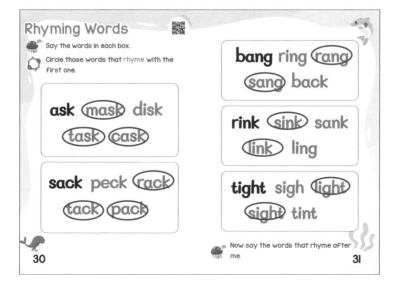

Rhyming Words

Say the words in each box.

Circle those words that rhyme with the first one.

ask (mask) disk (task) (cask)

sack peck (rack) (tack) (pack)

bang ring (rang) (sang) back

rink (sink) sank (link) ling

tight sigh (light) (sight) tint

Now say the words that rhyme after me.

30

31

133

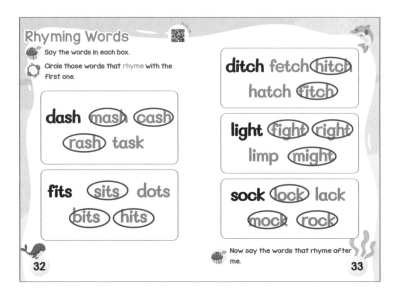

Rhyming Words

Say the words in each box.

Circle those words that rhyme with the first one.

dash (mash) (cash) (rash) task

fits (sits) dots (bits) (hits)

ditch fetch (hitch) hatch (fitch)

light (fight) (right) limp (might)

sock (lock) lack (mock) (rock)

Now say the words that rhyme after me.

32   33

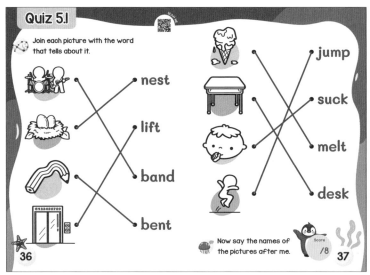

Quiz 5.1

Join each picture with the word that tells about it.

nest

lift

band

bent

jump

suck

melt

desk

Now say the names of the pictures after me.

Score /8

36   37

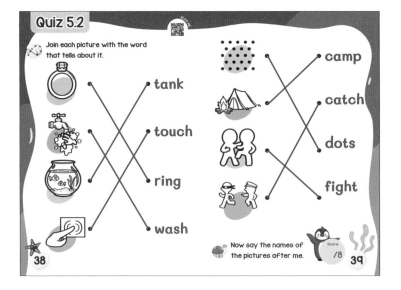

Quiz 5.2

Join each picture with the word that tells about it.

tank

touch

ring

wash

camp

catch

dots

fight

Now say the names of the pictures after me.

Score /8

38   39

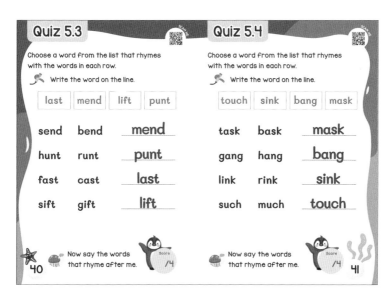

Quiz 5.3

Choose a word from the list that rhymes with the words in each row.

Write the word on the line.

| last | mend | lift | punt |

send	bend	__mend__
hunt	runt	__punt__
fast	cast	__last__
sift	gift	__lift__

Now say the words that rhyme after me.

Score /4

40

Quiz 5.4

Choose a word from the list that rhymes with the words in each row.

Write the word on the line.

| touch | sink | bang | mask |

task	bask	__mask__
gang	hang	__bang__
link	rink	__sink__
such	much	__touch__

Now say the words that rhyme after me.

Score /4

41

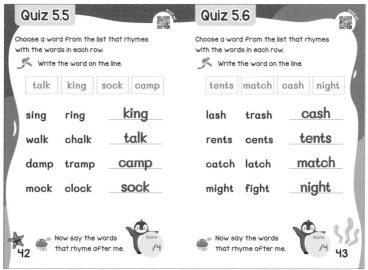

Quiz 5.5

Choose a word from the list that rhymes with the words in each row.

Write the word on the line.

| talk | king | sock | camp |

sing	ring	__king__
walk	chalk	__talk__
damp	tramp	__camp__
mock	clock	__sock__

Now say the words that rhyme after me.

Score /4

42

Quiz 5.6

Choose a word from the list that rhymes with the words in each row.

Write the word on the line.

| tents | match | cash | night |

lash	trash	__cash__
rents	cents	__tents__
catch	latch	__match__
might	fight	__night__

Now say the words that rhyme after me.

Score /4

43

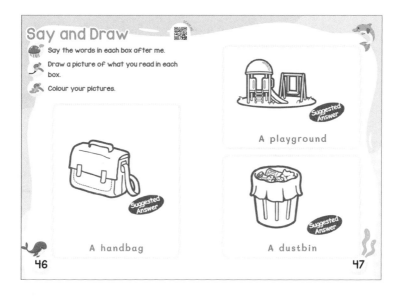

Say and Draw

Say the words in each box after me.

Draw a picture of what you read in each box.

Colour your pictures.

A playground

Suggested Answer

A handbag

Suggested Answer

A dustbin

Suggested Answer

46

47

135

Say and Draw

Say the words in each box after me.

Draw a picture of what you read in each box.

Colour your pictures.

A big doll

48

A fat pig

A long belt

49

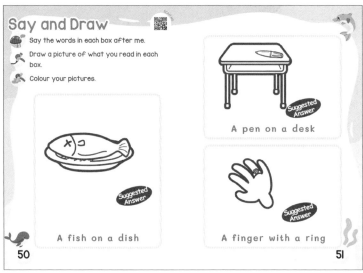

Say and Draw

Say the words in each box after me.

Draw a picture of what you read in each box.

Colour your pictures.

A fish on a dish

50

A pen on a desk

A finger with a ring

51

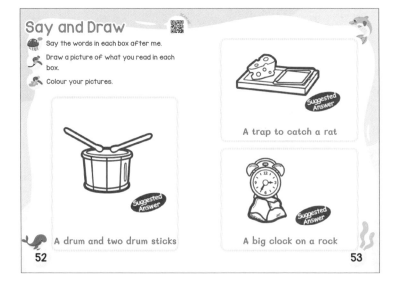

Say and Draw

Say the words in each box after me.

Draw a picture of what you read in each box.

Colour your pictures.

A drum and two drum sticks

52

A trap to catch a rat

A big clock on a rock

53

136

Say and Draw

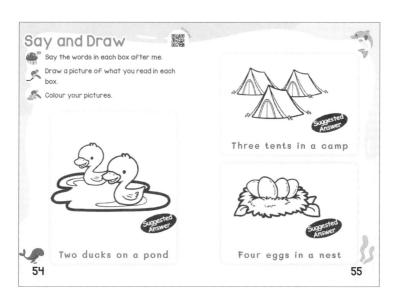

🦑 Say the words in each box after me.

🐙 Draw a picture of what you read in each box.

🐌 Colour your pictures.

Three tents in a camp

Suggested Answer

Two ducks on a pond

Suggested Answer

Four eggs in a nest

Suggested Answer

54

55

Riddles

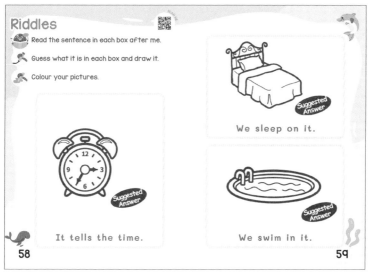

🦑 Read the sentence in each box after me.

🐙 Guess what it is in each box and draw it.

🐌 Colour your pictures.

We sleep on it.

Suggested Answer

It tells the time.

Suggested Answer

We swim in it.

Suggested Answer

58

59

Riddles

🦑 Read the sentence in each box after me.

🐙 Guess what it is in each box and draw it.

🐌 Colour your pictures.

We use it to catch fish.

Suggested Answer

We need it when it rains.

Suggested Answer

We get it from the bank.

Suggested Answer

60

61

137

Riddles

- Read the sentence in each box after me.
- Guess what it is in each box and draw it.
- Colour your pictures.

Suggested Answer

He wears a crown.

62

It lives in the sea.

Suggested Answer

Suggested Answer

We beat it to make sounds.

63

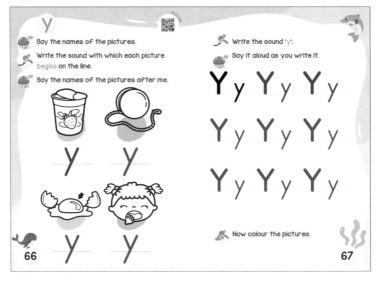

y

- Say the names of the pictures.
- Write the sound with which each picture begins on the line.
- Say the names of the pictures after me.

y   y

y   y

66

- Write the sound 'y'.
- Say it aloud as you write it.

Y y Y y Y y

Y y Y y Y y

Y y Y y Y y

- Now colour the pictures.

67

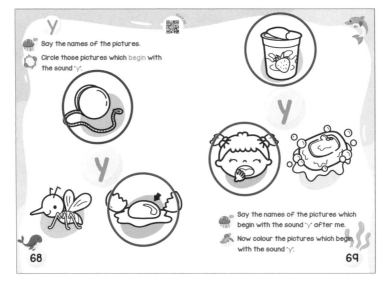

y

- Say the names of the pictures.
- Circle those pictures which begin with the sound 'y'.

y

y

y

- Say the names of the pictures which begin with the sound 'y' after me.
- Now colour the pictures which begin with the sound 'y'.

68

69

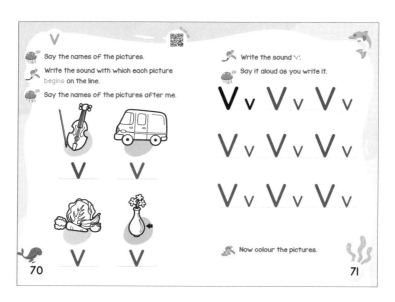

Say the names of the pictures.

Write the sound with which each picture begins on the line.

Say the names of the pictures after me.

V V V V

Write the sound 'v'.

Say it aloud as you write it.

V v V v V v
V v V v V v
V v V v V v

Now colour the pictures.

70

71

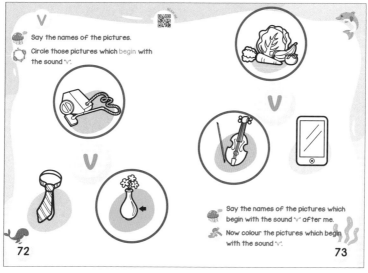

Say the names of the pictures.

Circle those pictures which begin with the sound 'v'.

Say the names of the pictures which begin with the sound 'v' after me.

Now colour the pictures which begin with the sound 'v'.

72

73

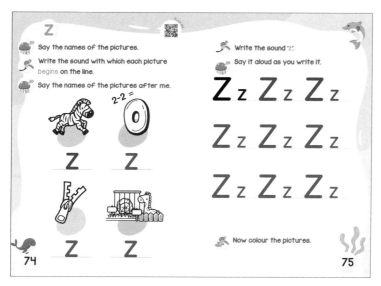

Say the names of the pictures.

Write the sound with which each picture begins on the line.

Say the names of the pictures after me.

2-2 =

Z Z Z Z

Write the sound 'z'.

Say it aloud as you write it.

Z z Z z Z z
Z z Z z Z z
Z z Z z Z z

Now colour the pictures.

74

75

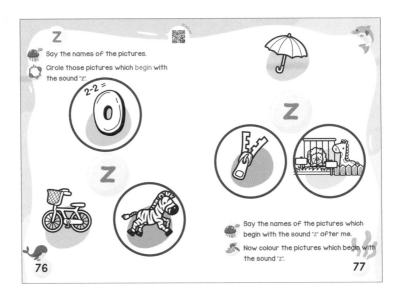

z

Say the names of the pictures.

Circle those pictures which begin with the sound 'z'.

2-2 =

Say the names of the pictures which begin with the sound 'z' after me.

Now colour the pictures which begin with the sound 'z'.

76

77

qu

Say the names of the pictures.

Write the sound with which each picture begins on the line.

Say the names of the pictures after me.

qu   qu

qu   qu

Write the sound 'qu'.

Say it aloud as you write it.

Qu qu   Qu qu

Qu qu   Qu qu

Qu qu   Qu qu

Now colour the pictures.

78

79

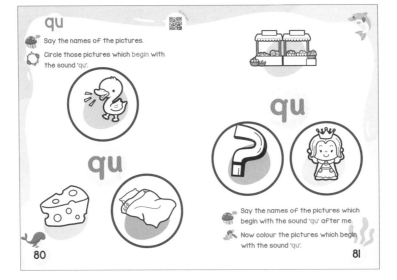

qu

Say the names of the pictures.

Circle those pictures which begin with the sound 'qu'.

qu

qu

Say the names of the pictures which begin with the sound 'qu' after me.

Now colour the pictures which begin with the sound 'qu'.

80

81

140

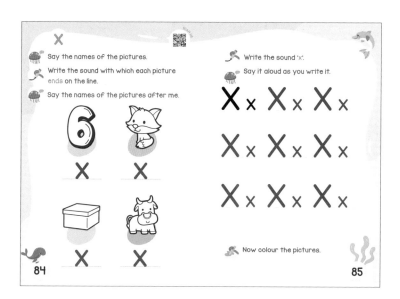

Page 84

X

Say the names of the pictures.

Write the sound with which each picture ends on the line.

Say the names of the pictures after me.

6 X

box X

84

Page 85

Write the sound 'x'.

Say it aloud as you write it.

X x X x X x

X x X x X x

X x X x X x

Now colour the pictures.

85

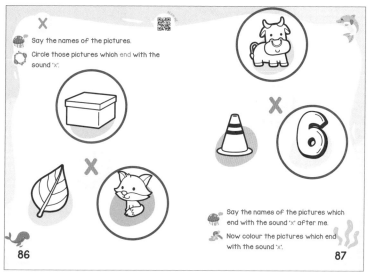

Page 86

X

Say the names of the pictures.

Circle those pictures which end with the sound 'x'.

86

Page 87

Say the names of the pictures which end with the sound 'x' after me.

Now colour the pictures which end with the sound 'x'.

87

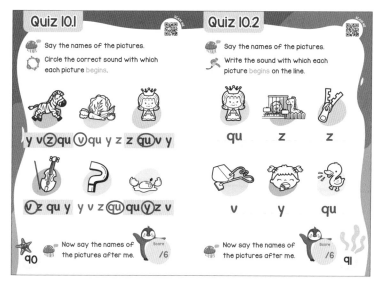

Quiz 10.1

Say the names of the pictures.

Circle the correct sound with which each picture begins.

y v z qu   v qu y z   z qu v y

v z qu y   y v z qu   qu y z v

Now say the names of the pictures after me.   Score /6

90

Quiz 10.2

Say the names of the pictures.

Write the sound with which each picture begins on the line.

qu   z   z

v   y   qu

Now say the names of the pictures after me.   Score /6

91

141

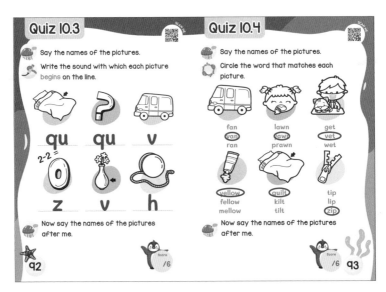

Quiz 10.3

Say the names of the pictures.

Write the sound with which each picture begins on the line.

qu **qu** **v**

z **v** **h**

Now say the names of the pictures after me.

Score /6

q2

Quiz 10.4

Say the names of the pictures.

Circle the word that matches each picture.

fan | lawn | get
van | **lawn** | **vet**
ran | prawn | wet

yellow | **quilt** | tip
fellow | kilt | lip
mellow | tilt | **zip**

Now say the names of the pictures after me.

Score /6

q3

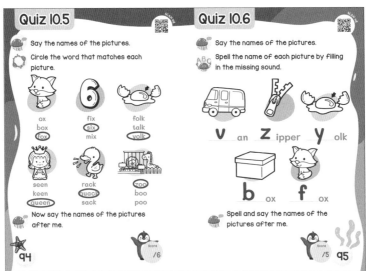

Quiz 10.5

Say the names of the pictures.

Circle the word that matches each picture.

ox | fix | folk
box | **six** | talk
fox | mix | **yolk**

seen | rack | **zoo**
keen | **quack** | boo
queen | sack | poo

Now say the names of the pictures after me.

Score /6

q4

Quiz 10.6

Say the names of the pictures.

Spell the name of each picture by filling in the missing sound.

v an **z** ipper **y** olk

b ox **f** ox

Spell and say the names of the pictures after me.

Score /5

q5

Quiz 10.7

Say the names of the pictures.

Spell the name of each picture by filling in the missing sound.

v iolin **y** o-yo **qu** een

o x **v** et

Spell and say the names of the pictures after me.

Score /5

q6

Quiz 10.8

Say the names of the pictures.

Spell the name of each picture by filling in the missing sound.

y awn **z** ero **v** ase

qu ack **z** oo

Spell and say the names of the pictures after me.

Score /5

q7

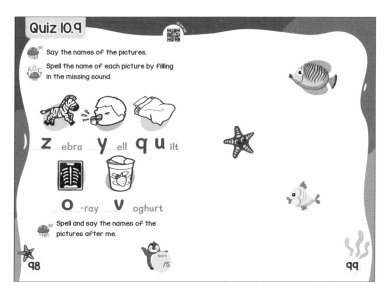

Quiz 10.9

Say the names of the pictures.

ABC Spell the name of each picture by filling in the missing sound.

z ebra   **y** ell   **q u** ilt

o -ray   **v** oghurt

Spell and say the names of the pictures after me.

98

Score /5

99

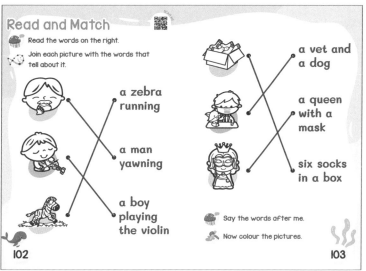

Read and Match

Read the words on the right.

Join each picture with the words that tell about it.

a zebra running

a man yawning

a boy playing the violin

a vet and a dog

a queen with a mask

six socks in a box

Say the words after me.

Now colour the pictures.

102

103

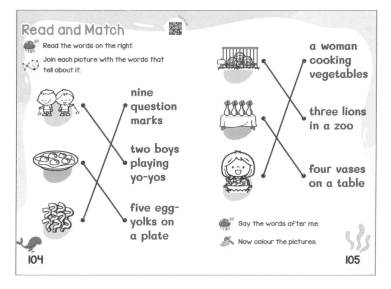

Read and Match

Read the words on the right.

Join each picture with the words that tell about it.

nine question marks

two boys playing yo-yos

five egg-yolks on a plate

a woman cooking vegetables

three lions in a zoo

four vases on a table

Say the words after me.

Now colour the pictures.

104

105

143

Read and Draw

Read the words in each box after me.

Draw as you are told to do.

Colour your pictures.

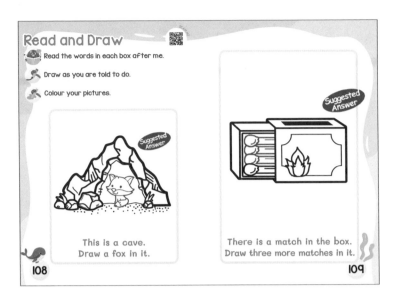

Suggested Answer

This is a cave.
Draw a fox in it.

108

Suggested Answer

There is a match in the box.
Draw three more matches in it.

109

Read and Draw

Read the words in each box after me.

Draw as you are told to do.

Colour your pictures.

Suggested Answer

It is raining.
Draw an umbrella for the man.

110

Suggested Answer

It is sunny.
Draw two birds flying in the sky.

111

Read and Draw

Read the words in each box after me.

Draw as you are told to do.

Colour your pictures.

Suggested Answer

Ann is very hungry.
Draw a hotdog on her plate.

112

Suggested Answer

Mother gives a bike to Tom.
Draw Tom riding on it.

113

Read and Draw

Scan me

🔊 Read the words in each box after me.

✏️ Draw as you are told to do.

🖍️ Colour your pictures.

This is a doll.
Colour her dress orange
and her hair yellow.

114

This is a clown.
Colour his nose red
and his hair green.

115

Riddles

🔊 Read the sentences in each box after me.

✏️ Guess the animal riddle and draw the answer in the box.

🔤 Spell the name of the animal and write it on the lines.

🖍️ Colour your pictures.

a **c a t**
It has big eyes and a long tail.
It says, "Meow, meow!"

118

a **d u c k**
It swims on a pond.
It says, "Quack, quack!"

119

Riddles

🔊 Read the sentences in each box after me.

✏️ Guess the animal riddle and draw the answer in the box.

🔤 Spell the name of the animal and write it on the lines.

🖍️ Colour your pictures.

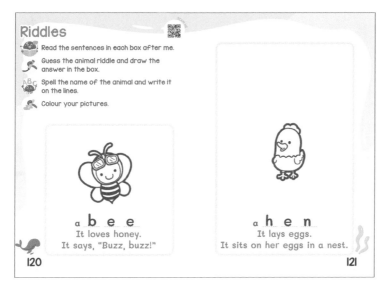

a **b e e**
It loves honey.
It says, "Buzz, buzz!"

120

a **h e n**
It lays eggs.
It sits on her eggs in a nest.

121

145

Riddles

- Read the sentences in each box after me.
- Guess the animal riddle and draw the answer in the box.
- Spell the name of the animal and write it on the lines.
- Colour your pictures.

a <u>h o r s e</u>
It has four legs.
It is strong and fast. We can ride on it.

122

a <u>f r o g</u>
It has a green skin.
It can jump and swim in the pond.

123

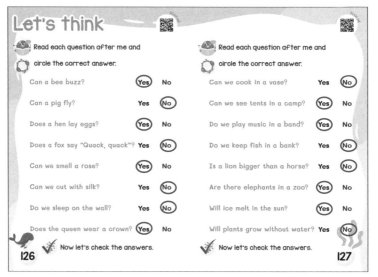

Let's think

- Read each question after me and circle the correct answer.

Can a bee buzz?	(Yes) No
Can a pig fly?	Yes (No)
Does a hen lay eggs?	(Yes) No
Does a fox say "Quack, quack"?	Yes (No)
Can we smell a rose?	(Yes) No
Can we cut with silk?	Yes (No)
Do we sleep on the wall?	Yes (No)
Does the queen wear a crown?	(Yes) No

Now let's check the answers.

126

- Read each question after me and circle the correct answer.

Can we cook in a vase?	Yes (No)
Can we see tents in a camp?	(Yes) No
Do we play music in a band?	(Yes) No
Do we keep fish in a bank?	Yes (No)
Is a lion bigger than a horse?	Yes (No)
Are there elephants in a zoo?	(Yes) No
Will ice melt in the sun?	(Yes) No
Will plants grow without water?	Yes (No)

Now let's check the answers.

127